TELL ME
A STORY
BEFORE I GO TO BED

Pour Jeanne, S.B.

First published in hardback in Great Britain as *Up the Wooden Hill*
by HarperCollins Children's Books in 2005
First published in paperback in 2006

1 3 5 7 9 10 8 6 4 2

ISBN-13: 978-0-00-780282-1

HarperCollins Children's Books is a division of HarperCollins Publishers Ltd.

Text copyright © Sam McBratney 2005
Illustrations copyright © Sebastien Braun 2005

The author and illustrator assert the moral right to be identified as the author and illustrator of the work.

A CIP catalogue record is available from the British Library.

Visit our website at: www.harpercollinschildrensbooks.co.uk

Printed and bound in Malaysia

Something with steps.

Something with creaky steps…

A thing made of wood and not too far away…

And she went up it every night to bed…

And on her daddy's back.

"I *do* know what it is!" Anna-Sophia cried, all of a sudden.
"It's the stairs. The wooden hill is just our stairs.
They always make a creaking noise and I go up
them to bed and they're made of wood."
It was a great guess! Her mum was so pleased
to hear the right answer that she clapped her hands.

"Here's one more clue," her daddy said. "It's got steps. It creaks when you walk on it and you go up the wooden hill every night to bed."

Anna-Sophia thought...

and thought...

...and then thought some more.

Anna-Sophia lived in a quiet part of the
woods, not so far from here. She lived
in a grand big house with an upstairs
and a downstairs and lots of places
to play hide and seek.

TELL ME A STORY

BEFORE I GO TO BED

BY SAM MCBRATNEY

ILLUSTRATED BY SEBASTIEN BRAUN

HarperCollins *Children's Books*

She thought about the hill behind their house –
but that was a hill of grass and flowers and
definitely not made of wood.

"Where is the wooden hill?" asked Anna-Sophia.

"See if you can guess," said Dad.

"I'll give you a clue – it's not far from here."

Anna-Sophia began to think.

Oh well, she said to herself. Mummy and Daddy often
said things that she didn't understand, so perhaps the
wooden hill was just another one of those.

Or could he mean the slide in the park,
which was another thing that you could go up…

She loved to climb up and down
the crooked tree in the orchard to
see how the apples were growing.
Perhaps her daddy meant that.
It was certainly made of *wood*.

"Will you carry me up to bed on your back?" she asked.

"I certainly will," said her dad, supping the last of his stew.

"I'll carry you on my back all the way up the wooden hill."

"What is the wooden hill?" asked Anna-Sophia.

"Here's another clue to help you think –
you go up and down it every day."

Anna-Sophia thought and thought…

One evening, Anna-Sophia got ready for bed in front
of the fire. Her mum combed her hair while her
daddy ate his dinner. He wasn't long in from the
fields and said he was so hungry that he
could eat a horse.

It was also quite an old house,
which meant that some of the floorboards
creaked when you walked on them.
Anna-Sophia loved to play hide and seek…
especially up and down the creaky stairs.

"I certainly will," he said. Her dad knew lots of stories.
He knew so many that he hardly ever told the same
one twice. "I'll tell you a story when we go
up the wooden hill."

"Will you tell me a story, Daddy?"
said Anna-Sophia.

Could he mean the wooden bridge
over the frozen lake? Surely not!
Anna-Sophia felt cold just
thinking about it.

"Indeed I will," said her dad. "I'll tuck you in as tight as you like when we go up the wooden hill."

"But where *is* the wooden hill?" asked Anna-Sophia.

"Daddy – will you tuck me in when I go up to bed on your back?" she asked.

...and down?

I don't know much about
wooden hills, thought
Anna-Sophia.